I Saw an Ant on the Railroad Track

For my little ants, Noah, Ivy, and Maisie -J.P.

For Mom, Dad, and Aymone. Thanks to Dexter and
that dreamy place called Davao -M.P.

Library of Congress Cataloging-in-Publication Data

Prince, Joshua.
I saw an ant on the railroad track / Joshua Prince; illustrated by Macky Pamintuan.
p. cm.
Summary: Jack, a railroad switchman, frantically tries to save an ant who is heading east on a westbound
track, straight into the path of an oncoming freight train.
ISBN 1-4027-2183-8
[1. Ants—Fiction. 2. Railroads—Fiction. 3. Stories in rhyme.] I. Pamintuan, Macky, ill. II. Title.

PZ8.3.P934Ias 2006
[E]—dc22
2005018997

1 2 3 4 5 6 7 8 9 10

Published by Sterling Publishing Co., Inc.
387 Park Avenue South, New York, NY 10016
Text copyright © 2006 by Joshua Prince
Illustrations copyright © 2006 by Macky Pamintuan
Designed by Randall Heath
Distributed in Canada by Sterling Publishing
c/o Canadian Manda Group, 165 Dufferin Street
Toronto, Ontario, Canada M6K 3H6
Distributed in Great Britain and Europe by Chris Lloyd at Orca Book
Services, Stanley House, Fleets Lane, Poole BH15 3AJ, England
Distributed in Australia by Capricorn Link (Australia) Pty. Ltd.
P.O. Box 704, Windsor, NSW 2756, Australia

Sterling ISBN-13: 978-1-4027-4231-6
ISBN-10: 1-4027-4231-2

For information about custom editions, special sales, premium and
corporate purchases, please contact Sterling Special Sales
Department at 800-805-5489 or specialsales@sterlingpub.com.

ABOUT THE AUTHOR AND THE ILLUSTRATOR

Joshua Prince lives in Westport, Connecticut, but rides a train daily to his
life as an advertising writer in New York. A brief encounter with an ant at
his regular station inspired this story, which is his first book. He is married
with three children.

Born and raised in the Philippines, Macky Pamintuan's parents discovered
early on that giving him paper and a pencil was a sure way to keep him busy,
quiet, and out of trouble. Macky moved to San Francisco and enrolled in the
Academy of Art College. He has received a grant award at the Society of
Illustrators Annual Scholarship Competition.

I Saw an Ant on the Railroad Track

By **Joshua Prince**

Illustrated by **Macky Pamintuan**

Sterling Publishing Co., Inc.

New York

Well, I saw an ant on the railroad track.
The rail was bright.
The ant was black.
He was walking along, *tickety-tack*.
(That's the sound of an ant on a railroad track.)

Now this little ant was in search of a snack,
  an eastbound ant
  on a westbound track,
looking for a crumb or a nut to crack
  on the shiny bright rail of a railroad track.

And who am I? I'm switchman Jack,
just working my shift
in the switchman's shack.
I switch the trains from track to track
as east goes west and forth goes back.

I'd just settled down with my brown lunch sack,
   napkin spread,
   lunch unpacked,
when I spied that ant on the railroad track,
   hungry, hunting, *tickety-tack*.

So we lunched together,
ant
and
Jack.